Large Print Edition

Rescue

A Litter of Quetzels

A.B. Richards

PUBLISHED BY:
Black Mare Books
Houston, Texas
www.blackmarebooks.com

ISBN: 978-1-941502-33-4

Rescue: A Litter of Quetzels

Contents

Prey

"Hello," said the man to the little girl. She was playing with her twin brother out on the well-groomed front lawn of their suburban home. A little black kitten chased clumsily after a catnip mouse tied to a piece of string that they took turns dragging around the yard. The front door was open, but there was no adult to be seen.

The children were achingly beautiful. They had huge blue eyes and hair like sun on the beach in summer. They couldn't have been older than five.

"Hello," the girl answered, bowing her head a little and looking up through her thick lashes.

He smiled at her, craving her. "Where's your mommy, sugar?" He stretched his hand toward her.

"I'm right here." A tall woman with the same blue eyes and blonde hair stood in the doorway, arms crossed.

The man turned and pulled back his hand, squelching a scowl.

"Is there something I can help you with?" the woman asked.

"Oh. I just saw the children alone. I was just making sure they were all right."

"Of course you were." She bared her teeth in more of a snarl than a smile. "A piece of advice - don't meddle with things that don't belong to you. Envy is a deadly sin."

The man left. But he began to watch the house. He planned, smeared mud on his license plate so it couldn't be read. Bought a wig. It took a few days, but he finally saw his chance. The children were out in the yard again, playing with the kitten.

He pulled up to the curb in front of the house and got out of the car, leaving the engine running. He opened the passenger door, then scooped up the little girl, cat and all, and threw her in the car. He took off, as fast as he could without screeching the tires, leaving the little boy staring after them as they disappeared down the street.

The man's hands shook on the steering wheel, adrenalin pounding through his veins. He looked at his prize. She gazed out the window, humming something, and he couldn't quite catch the tune. The kitten yowled occasionally. But he wasn't really listening. He was thinking what he would do with this fantastic, beautiful child. He drove her out to an abandoned house in the country. He had taken a little girl there once before. Even though he'd gotten caught, caught before he could do what he wanted, he still liked the location.

When they arrived, he opened the door for her and took her hand.

She looked at him with Japanime eyes and an almost smile. "Are you planning to hurt me?"

Her question rattled him. Not knowing how he should answer, he just grunted. It was like she knew what he was planning, and she wasn't afraid of him. The man did not like this sharing of power. It should, in his opinion, be all or nothing, with him having all and her having nothing.

He locked her and her stupid kitten in the back bedroom and paced around the house, trying to think, rotting floorboards creaking under his feet. He needed her fear to squash down the fear inside himself, to feel powerful. Angry now, he strode to the bedroom. There was no electricity in the old farmhouse and there wasn't that much daylight left. Hurrying, he opened the door.

"Little girl," he crooned, "come and get a surprise."

But the girl was gone.

There was nothing in the room but a broken chair and some trash. The window was closed and locked. He looked in the closet. There was nothing there. Then he heard laughter. A child's laughter. He turned around and saw a flash of motion by the door.

"Dammit." How had she gotten past him? He ran to the door and heard another door slam. He raced through the house. Every door he saw was shut. "Ollie ollie oxen free! Come out, come out wherever you are," he called, in his silkiest voice.

He heard more childish laughter. "Come and find me!"

Anger twisted its way up through his solar plexus, up to his chest and face. This was not going the way he had planned at all. He was supposed to be the boss. It wasn't fair.

"Come here right now! Don't be so naughty," he shouted.

His answer was the creaking of the spring on the screen door and the slap of the door on the frame.

He swore to himself as he ran outside. He saw legs and hair disappearing around the corner of the decaying garage. Surely he could run down a five year old child. Now he had her. He rounded the corner and saw an open field. There was no one to be seen, just the blood-red light of the dying sun. No hiding places, no trampled grass, nothing. He stalked around the garage. The oppressively sweet smell of honeysuckle assaulted him.

Then he saw her.

She was sitting with her back to him, moving back and forth slowly on a decrepit swing hanging from an overgrown oak tree. The chain skreaked, rusty metal on rusty metal as she swung. He crept up behind her, all stealth and malice. Gloating, he grabbed her shoulder.

"Gotcha!"

Unexpectedly, and lighting fast, she bit his hand. He yelped and let go. He raised his hand to strike her, then froze as he saw her face.

The lovely peaches and cream skin was now green and scaly, reptilian. Her spectacular blue eyes were yellow, almost glowing, and her pupils were vertical slits. A thin, forked tongue flicked out over vicious serrated teeth and licked her hard lips. She laughed again, a sweet and horrible child's laugh. The kitten sat in her lap, unperturbed. He wanted to grab that kitten and wring its neck. That would show her.

Then he felt it. His blood was on fire. Venom spread up his arm from the bite wound. He screamed and clutched at his shoulder. "What did you do to me?" he rasped.

The burning spread into his chest and he fell to his knees. The lizard girl sat in the swing and sang *Freré*

Jaques in her angel's voice. He had come out here so no one could the screams.

He hadn't counted on the screams being his own.

He writhed in agony in the dirt and dead grass. Then his muscles started to tighten up. He couldn't move. He couldn't speak. The burning lessened, merely painful now instead of unbearable.

The thing in the shape of a girl approached him, mouth open, breath hissing. She crouched near his leg, keeping her amber eyes on his. The kitten sat beside her, licking its whiskers.

"Tsk, tsk. Mother did warn you, after all."

Even though he couldn't move, he could feel.

Everything.

He felt each individual tooth as it sliced into his leg. He felt the hunk of muscle tear away. He saw his own blood on the lips of his would-be victim, watched her chew his flesh as she devoured him alive. Pain and horror overcame him, and he slipped into oblivion.

Two FBI agents from the Behavior Analysis Unit stood near Detective Quetzel Cazares, next to a rusty swing. A Texas Ranger spoke to the coroner, clipboard in hand, taking notes.

"Looks like we've got a vigilante," the detective said. "Targets sex offenders."

"Maybe. What's the count? Seven? These offenders, though. All lived in the same zip code, and all their victims were juveniles," said the FBI agent in the blue tie.

"This one may be number eight. Same MO," said the agent in the red tie.

"Quetz, you come over here?" called Cooper Morgenstern, from the Medical Examiner's office.

"What've you got, Coop?"

Morgenstern squatted down by a bloody skeleton. Tattered ribbons of drying flesh festooned the bones. Flies buzzed around, hopeful of finding something soft.

"I can tell you this was a male. Judging by the amount of blood around him, he was alive when this happened. No

ID, but if he's a registered sex offender like the others, we should get a DNA hit on CODIS."

"Yeah," said Cazares to both the agents and Morgenstern. "A sheriff's deputy saw the car parked outside this old farmhouse and ran the plates. Found out it belonged to Michael Dwayne Harris, a known sex offender. We'll just have to see if the bones belong to him, too."

Cazares eyed the grisly remains. He must have died an awful death. But she had seen his case file, and she had trouble summoning up much pity for him.

🐈

Back in the suburbs, the splendidly beautiful children sat next to their mother on the couch, looking at a laptop computer screen. The little black kitten snoozed in the girl's lap.

"You cannot keep him," the mother said, shaking her head at her daughter.

"Why not?" The girl's lower lip trembled and her huge eyes welled with tears.

"He eats too much. My decision is final. I have already put an ad for him on craigslist."

The girl clutched the kitten to her chest, and he protested half-heartedly.

"Look, my darlings," the mother purred.

They were looking at the database entries for sex offenders in their zip code.

"Let's check the menu, shall we? I don't know what it is about these people that makes them so extra tasty. Perhaps it is fear. They are soaked in it." She scrolled through the listings, looking for entries marked 'Indecency W/A Child.'

The mother pouted. "We shall have to move soon - there are only three of the sort we like left in this area. Look, one of these delectable meals lives at the apartment complex just down the road. My, he's especially plump and juicy. Perhaps I shall have him for myself."

"No. You must share, Mother, especially that one," said the little boy, licking his lips.

Gone to the Dogs

Detective Quetzel Cazares peered into the sodden duffle bag. It contained a torso, two legs, and one and a half arms, sans hands. The jagged edges of flesh had faded to an ashy grey from being submerged in the pond.

"Gang related?" asked the patrol officer who'd answered the call.

"Well, you know this part of town. Probably. But he's not inked, at least not what I can see of his arms. What's the story here? I think the dispatcher was on cold meds or something when I got the call – I couldn't understand half of what she said."

The officer, D. Chan, according to his name tag, said, "Kid's birthday party. The dad," he paused to look at his report, "Franklin Williams, brought his son and five of his friends to go fishing in the retention pond here at the park.

Thought they'd caught a big turtle." He glanced down at the canvas bag.

Cazares shook her head. "Did they look inside?"

Chan nodded.

She grimaced. "Poor kids."

The Crime Scene Unit arrived and invaded the park like white jump-suited ants.

"I hope they get a DNA hit. I've got no prints, no dental records, and no missing persons that even remotely match Mr. Doe here."

"Detective?" called another officer as he jogged up to the crime scene. "I think you should see this."

Cazares followed him to an unmowed area around a stand of Loblolly pine trees. Blue-bottle flies swarmed around the stiff body of a medium-sized brown dog that lay in the weeds. Several rounds of duct tape had been wound around its muzzle. The poor animal was covered in ragged wounds and puncture marks. But one injury stood out. The dog's throat gaped open, and the severed trachea lapped the grass like a grotesque tongue. The eye on the visible side of its head was missing.

"This is the third one we've found this month," the officer said.

That brought Cazares up short. Serial killers often practiced on animals before they upgraded to humans. On the other hand, it could just be a rotten coincidence.

"Good catch," she said, nodding. "I'll tell CSU to come over here. Maybe they can connect these two. Or maybe not."

There weren't likely to be any recoverable fingerprints on the dog, but there might be on the duct tape. Even if the dog dumper wasn't connected to the dismembered corpse in the duffle bag, that person was a sick individual and who needed be caught.

"Looks like a bait dog," the officer said.

"Bait dog?"

"Yeah," he replied, shaking his head. "When they train dogs to fight, they use dogs or other animals that have been...disabled. Lot of free puppies or free kittens end up inside a pit bull."

There wasn't much that surprised the homicide detective. But this did. "Too many turds in the world," she said.

The officer nodded.

Cazares made her way back over to the duffle bag by the lake. She looked for any evidence of something being dragged between the pond and the trees - flattened grass, scrape marks on the gravel trail, traces of blood. But she saw nothing remarkable – the grass was too short and the path too gravelly and dry. Hopefully, the Medical Examiner could give her more information, because right now, she had squat.

So far, the ME's office had not been able to identify the body. All of the pieces did belong to the same corpse, so that was a plus. There were fragments of a tattoo on the back of the neck where the head had been severed, but not enough to determine what it might have been. The victim was a young male, approximately twenty, and there were two point-blank gunshot wounds to the chest. There was no alcohol or controlled substances found, but between the decomp and being submerged in the pond, the tests may not have been accurate.

Cazares pinned the pictures from the coroner's office up on her cube wall, next to ones from the crime scene. The CSU had been able to recover a latent print on the duct tape, but there were no matches from the AFIS database yet. There was nothing to connect the deaths of the man and the dog, either, but Cazares had a hunch that they were somehow related.

She was just about to leave for a late lunch when she got a call from the ME's office.

"Quetz?" It was Cooper Morgenstern.

"Hey, Coop. What have you got for me?"

"Just wanted to let you know that we haven't had any CODIS hits on the DNA."

"You're calling to tell me that?" Cazares cut in, grumpy from low blood sugar.

"No. I'm calling to tell you that we did find something. The decedent had Trisomy 21. Down's Syndrome."

"Really?" she said. Sad as that may be, it was the first solid lead in the whole case. "Thanks for letting me know, Coop."

"No prob," Morgenstern said and hung up.

The garage used to be an auto repair shop. But as the surrounding neighborhood decayed, so did the business. By the time Chris Thompson's father had handed the shop down to him and his brother, the enterprise cost more money to operate than it brought in. To put food on the table, and take care of his handicapped younger brother, Dewey, Chris had to change his business model.

Now, he made more than his father had ever dreamed of making.

Chris had just finished hosing down the dog pens, and the smooth concrete floor was treacherous. He opened a pet crate and took out one of the two kittens inside. It was a pretty silver tabby with large green eyes. He'd found it, and its companion, on craigslist, along with all the others that had preceded them. He only chose the "shots & wormed, free to good home" ones. Didn't want to risk passing something nasty on to his dogs.

He tossed it casually into a reinforced pen with his new fighting dog. Chris watched impassively as the kitten fluffed its fur and hissed at the dog. But it never stood a chance. Its angry screech was silenced in mid-yowl as steel trap jaws snapped around its small form, severing its front legs and head from the rest of the body. Chris smiled to himself. This dog was something else, the best dog he'd ever had. In fact, the dog was so vicious that he was afraid to get in the pen with it, so he used a cattle prod to get it in and out of its crate.

The tiny cat had been reduced to a few bloody scraps of fur. Chris reached into the crate for the last kitten, a little black one.

"No!"

He turned to see Dewey standing in the doorway.

"I know you don't like it, bro. But I've got to train the dogs so we can have money for your medicine and to buy food."

Chris whirled as the kitten's needle-sharp teeth sank into his thumb. "Son of a bitch!" he shouted, as he jerked his hand out of the cage and put his thumb into his mouth.

The metal door clanked against the plastic crate as the kitten bolted for freedom. He cursed it and turned back to his brother.

"See what you've done, Dewey? I love you, but you're a total fuck-up, bro."

Dewey's overly round eyes glared defiantly from behind his thick glasses. "Bad Chris!" he shouted.

"Yeah, well Bad Chris is the only person who gives a shit about you, so maybe you can just shut up and get out of the way while I catch this damn cat."

Dewey refused to leave, and he started toward Chris. Unfortunately, he'd always been somewhat top-heavy, and when he slipped on the wet concrete, disaster struck. He tried to catch himself on the waist-high edge of the reinforced dog pen, but hit it too hard and low, flipping over the top and onto the chain link overhang, just like a prison fence minus the razor wire, that slanted inward and kept the dogs from jumping out.

Chris breathed a sigh of relief.

As Dewey started to move, the chain link collapsed under his weight and sent him tumbling into the pen.

"Fuck!" Chris shouted, and ran for the electric cattle prod.

"Here, doggie." Dewey reached out his hand to the dog.

Many other dogs would have viewed this as a friendly invitation. But not Chris' new dog. It sat there for a moment or two, drool hanging in slimy stalactites from its wide jaws. Then it lurched at Dewey, tripping over its own feet, before it seized him by the forearm and shook it back and forth.

The arm dislocated first at the shoulder, and then at the elbow, and Dewey screamed in fear and pain. Blood flowed like a bathtub faucet out of his arm as the vicious teeth punctured and crushed blood vessels.

"I'm comin'! Hang on!" Chris shouted.

He grabbed the cattle prod off the top of the pet crate and ran to the pen. Mashing the power button, he shoved the hotshot through the fence and hit the dog in the flank. The prod was dead, no charge. He let loose every curse word he knew, and then invented some more. In desperation, he leaned over the broken fence and started beating the dog's broad head with the cattle prod.

The animal let go of Dewey's arm long enough to snap at the fiberglass stick. It missed, then re-clamped his jaws on Dewey's head. He screamed louder as his glasses shattered. Teeth and glass drove into his eye socket. Dewey clawed at his face with his good arm, and the dog grabbed his wrist in response.

Chris rained down blows on the beast until the cattle prod snapped in two and one end went flying.

"Get off! Get off!" he alternately begged and screamed at the beast.

A dark blur caught Chris's eye. The black kitten with the tiny white spot on its chest, the one he had intended to throw to the dog just minutes earlier, had jumped up on the edge of the pen.

"Mew?" it said.

The dog stopped shaking Dewey and looked up.

The kitten fluffed its tail and hissed.

The dog let go of his victim and lunged at the wall. The kitten sat and licked its paw, undisturbed by the shuddering boards underneath it. Then it rubbed its ears with the newly cleaned foot. The enraged dog snarled and flung itself at the barrier, foam flying from its mouth and spattering the wood and steel, trying to bite the chain link that separated it from the tiny cat.

While the kitten was busy ignoring the ravening dog, Chris dragged his brother out of the pen. Dewey was in a bad way. Part of his skull was caved in, and blood ran down his face from his ruined eye like rusty tears. He didn't have the strength to scream any more, just whimper. Dewey was dying, nothing could stop that now. And he was suffering horribly.

Chris sobbed as he pulled the Glock from his waistband. "Oh, God, Dewey. I'm so sorry. I'm so sorry."

He pointed the gun at the dog, which, oddly enough, was now cringing in the furthest corner of the pen, tail between its legs. Seconds ticked by, but Chris couldn't pull the trigger. The dog was his meal ticket, and if he shot it, he may as well shoot himself while he was at it.

Chris turned to back to his brother. Dewey made a heart-wrenching moan as his back arched and he writhed in agony.

"Dammit, Dewey. Dammit to hell," Chris said with tears streaming down his cheeks. The kindest thing he could do, he reckoned, was to hurry Dewey's inevitable end. Truth be told, it was the kindest thing he could do for himself, too. If the cops started poking around the shop, it wasn't going to end well for him.

The first shot missed. He had targeted Dewey's head, but he was shaking so hard that his aim was not even close. A window shattered as the bullet ricocheted off the concrete. Still bawling like a baby, Chris dropped to his knees and straddled his brother.

"I love you. Tell Mom I always tried to take care of you. I'm sorry. So fucking sorry."

He put the ugly barrel of the gun up against Dewey's chest and pulled the trigger. The force of the gunshot caused his brother's body to shake and buck, like a flag in storm. Blood and bone fragments spattered Chris' face and hands. But Dewey was still whimpering. Nearly blinded by tears, Chris shot his brother again.

This time, Dewey was still.

🐈

Detective Cazares sat at her desk, sipping a cup of cold coffee. She hadn't intended to drink it that way, but she didn't have time to go get a fresh cup. AFIS had finally come up with some suggestions for the latent fingerprint from the duct tape. Unfortunately, it was a partial, and there were several possible suspects. Of the five names it had generated, two were dead, one was in jail, and rap sheets for the other two lay on her desk. The first one,

Chris Thompson, was unremarkable – arrested once for shoplifting ten years ago as a juvenile, and had two speeding tickets over the last five years.

The other one was more promising. D'Marqis Johnson had been arrested for nearly everything except capital murder. She looked at his most recent mug shot. Sullen eyes stared out from a scarred face, covered in sores. *Meth or acne?* she wondered, shaking her head.

Her partner, Carl Louis, was still in the hospital, recovering from triple bypass surgery. She'd stop by and look in on him after work. Maybe pick up some takeout for his wife on the way. But she had to do something else first.

The partial print she had was not enough to get a search warrant. But D'Marqis had helpfully gotten himself arrested this morning for aggravated assault. She had an appointment to see him at County in fifteen.

"Hello, Mr. Johnson," Cazares chirped. "How are you doing this afternoon?" She usually got to be the "good cop."

"What do you want?" he asked without looking up. He was cuffed and shackled, slouched in a plastic chair that was bolted to the floor.

"I would like to show you some pictures, and maybe you can tell me a little bit about them." She smiled at him, but he never looked up at her face.

Cazares pulled a glossy 8 x 10 of the mutilated dog out of her folder and set it on the table. Johnson did not look directly at it, but his eyes strayed to the image. He pulled away from it and grimaced.

"What the hell? Why you showin' me sick shit like that?"

She didn't hold out much hope that the partial print on the duct tape belonged to him. He seemed too disturbed and surprised. But she pushed him, just to be sure.

"What was the dog's name?" she asked pleasantly.

"How the fuck should I know? I can't stand dogs."

"Hate them enough to kill them?" she asked.

"This ain't got nuthin' to do with me. Don't know why you even askin'." He hunched away from the table and the grisly photo on top of it, putting as much distance as possible between it and himself.

She figured he would be the sort to brag about what he'd done, if he'd done it. Besides, he was in for aggravated assault. An animal cruelty charge was the least of his worries, and lying about it wouldn't really make any real difference, penalty-wise, for the repeat offender. Cazares debated about showing him the second picture. She couldn't tie the dog to the body in the duffle bag, and it didn't seem very likely that Johnson had anything to do with the dog. The odds of randomly picking the killer out of today's arrests were likely to be much worse that winning the lotto. Still, you can't win if you don't buy a ticket.

"I'm going to show you another picture, and you can let me know if anything looks familiar."

She laid a full color photo of the remains from the duffle bag neatly on top of the dog photo.

Johnson retched and jerked his head away.

"I'll take that as a 'no.'" Cazares scooped the pictures back into her file folder. "Thank you for your time, Mr. Johnson. I hope you enjoy your stay here at the Hotel Harris County." She headed towards the door.

"Crazy bitch," Johnson growled after her.

If Quetzel hurried, she still had time to run down the other lead and go by the hospital. She had a patrol officer drive out to Chris Thompson's address with her. It may have been overkill, but if he was the killer, it would be stupid to go alone. She let Officer Reyes lead the way - so she could focus on turning the bits and pieces of her case over in her head, rather than looking for an address.

They pulled up into the wide driveway. Faded lettering on a cracked plastic sign read, "Thompson's Garage." The business itself was a rust-stained metal building with a dented aluminum garage door that was padlocked shut.

The office door next to it, however, was wide open.

🐈

Chris Thompson sat back on his heels and tucked the Glock back into his waistband. He was still straddling the bloody corpse of his brother.

"Oh, God, Dewey," he murmured as he rocked himself back and forth, face in his hands.

When he finally regained his composure, he stood up and assessed his predicament. His first thought was to call 911 and tell the police that he came back from the store and found Dewey on the floor like that. But the last thing he needed was a bunch of cops sniffing around his place. Where would he take the dogs? Not to mention his stash of weed and crank that he sold, concession-style, to the dogfight spectators.

He went into the bathroom and washed the blood off of his face, and pounded his fist on the wall next to the mirror. Any scenario that he could think of that would end with Dewey getting a proper burial next to their parents also included the police coming to the shop. He'd been so careful, never giving them a reason to notice him before.

"I'm so sorry, bro," he said to the corpse. "Please forgive me."

Chris went into his bedroom and rooted around in the closet until he found a large duffle bag. This was going to be the worst thing he'd ever done, and he hoped he could live with himself afterward. He set the bag down by Dewey's feet and picked up the hacksaw, hands shaking.

Chris weighted the duffle bag containing Dewey's body with a cinderblock so it wouldn't float when he dumped it in the pond. He also removed the remains of the bait dog that died a few days ago from the freezer. He'd leave that in the park, too. Just like the other two. When Chris returned at 3 AM, he was angry.

Angry with Dewey for falling into the dog pen.

Angry with himself for not being able to stop the dog attack.

Angry about what he'd been forced to do with his brother's body to try and keep himself out of trouble.

He wanted to hurt somebody.

So he decided to look for the kitten. Maybe murder by proxy would be good enough.

"Here, kitty, kitty," he called as he flipped the overhead lights on.

He noted, in passing, that the food in the new dog's dish was untouched. It was odd, because he kept his dogs hungry. They fought better that way. The dog sat in a corner of the pen, staring at him, eyes unusually bright. He chalked it up to the dog being disoriented by the lights coming on in the middle of the night.

"Kitty, kitty, kitty," he said again as he wandered into the far corner of the shop.

He heard the metallic thunk of the shop light switch being turned off behind him. He whirled to see green eyes glowing in the dark near the door. Green eyes about five feet above the ground, human height. But much larger than human.

A deep growl came from the direction of the eyes, then they began to come toward him.

Silently.

Quickly.

Chris panicked and fled toward the exit. He fumbled with the deadbolt and had managed to pull the door open before something huge hit him from behind, knocking him to the concrete walkway. He tried to cry out, but there was no air in his lungs. Sharp teeth penetrated his neck and back as the monster behind him picked him up by the scruff of his neck and dragged him back inside. If he moved, pain seared along his back and arms, so he remained as motionless as possible as he was hauled into the dark interior and towards the dog pens.

The already-flattened section of chain link groaned as the beast pulled Chris up onto it, then rolled him into the dog pen. He curled into a fetal position, waiting for the inevitable attack. Minutes passed, and nothing happened. He raised his head slightly to look around. His eyes had gotten used to the darkness again, and he could make out the form of the new dog staggering toward him. Its back nails scraped along the concrete, as if they were being dragged. The dog growled, then whined as it stood over him, head hanging low. Drool streamed onto Chris' face, running into his wounds and mixing with his blood.

The dog collapsed.

The creature that had dragged him into the pen had vanished. If not for the bloody wounds on his neck and shoulders, he might have been able to convince himself that he'd imagined the whole episode. He struggled out of the dog pen and turned on the lights.

The dog lay where it had fallen, eyes staring, breath rapid and shallow.

Chris was too drained to get angry again. But wasn't that just the way? First the dog, the best dog he's ever had, kills his brother. Now it tops that off by getting sick. It wasn't like Chris could take it to the vet. It would either live or die by its own strength. And it wasn't looking too strong right now.

It seemed to Chris that his life had suddenly taken a nosedive into the shit pile the day he picked up those last two kittens. The lady with the black kitten was hot, and he'd hoped she might want a little action, but she had two brats hanging around. His car broke down on the way home and he had to spend all of his cash to buy a part for it after he hiked over a mile to the auto parts store. Maybe black cats really were bad luck.

Chris took a shower and bandaged his injuries as best he could. He locked and barricaded his bedroom door against the green-eyed monster in the shop and fell into a fitful sleep, tucked into a corner behind the bed, Glock within easy reach.

🐈

Reyes and Cazares both drew their weapons as they carefully approached the open door of Thompson's Garage.

Cazares winkled her nose. The stench of feces and old blood wafting from inside was nauseating. This was not going to be good.

She stood to the side and knocked on the open door. "Hello? Anybody home?" she called into the darkness of the unlit shop.

There was no reply, but something clattered to the floor inside.

Reyes called for backup, then he pulled out his Maglite and held it next to his pistol as he peered around the edge of the door frame into the garage. A wooden pallet groaned against the concrete, and the boxes stacked on top of it wobbled.

The cardboard structure imploded. Out of the rubble, a man started crawling towards them. Saliva made a thin foam around his lower lip. Eyes sunken, he was dirty and disheveled.

Cazares and Reyes both took a step backward.

"Stop!" commanded Reyes.

The man continued towards them, babbling something that might have been "monster cat," but his mouth didn't seem to be working properly.

"I said stop! Down on the ground! Now!" shouted Reyes.

The man did not obey.

Cazares suddenly felt cold as recognition washed over her. She grabbed Reyes by the back of his Kevlar vest and hauled him out of the way, then slammed the door.

"Don't touch him!" she said through ragged breaths. "You don't want him to bleed, either. I've seen this before. Looks like rabies."

After the bio-hazard suited EMS personnel had taken the dying man away, after the five skeletal pit bulls had been picked up by Animal Control, after the Crime Scene Unit had arrived, Cazares leaned against the wall. The adrenalin that had kicked in earlier, when they first arrived at the garage, had gone and now she was bone tired. She wasn't going to make it by the hospital to see Carl tonight. But she, and everyone who showed up at the garage, had to start the rabies prophylaxis vaccine at the hospital later that morning.

She looked down as something brushed against her pant leg. A black kitten, ribs visible through its fluffy hair mewed hopefully at her.

"What are you doing here?" she asked as she picked it up. She felt sick as she remembered what Officer Chan had told her about dog fighters and free kittens.

The little cat purred, unexpectedly loudly for such a tiny thing, and kneaded her arm.

"You're hungry, aren't you?"

The kitten mewed again.

Animal control was long gone. The last thing she needed was a pet. But she didn't want to just leave it at the garage to starve. Aside from being skinny, the kitten appeared healthy. If it had rabies, it wasn't showing any symptoms. Besides, Quetzel had to get the shots anyway. She decided take the kitten home with her – there was leftover chicken in the fridge. She would feed the cat tonight and take it to the shelter tomorrow.

The kitten's eyes flickered green in the dark as it rode home in the detective's car, purring.

Lucky Cat

It was the brush of warm fur against her hand that startled her. When detective Quetzel Cazares woke up, she found the tiny black kitten that she'd rescued a few hours before curled up on her chest, underneath the covers. The little cat hardly weighed anything, maybe three pounds at the most, and when he realized she was awake, he began to knead her ribs with thin, sharp claws.

"I'd forgotten about you," Cazares said, petting the kitten.

He responded by stretching and purring.

"How about some breakfast, huh?"

She put her arm under the cat to support him when she stood up, and carried him into the kitchen. Her programmable coffee pot was already brewing her staple beverage. She didn't own a litter box, so she took him out into the backyard and set him down in one of her neglected flowerbeds. Cazares had planned to drop him off at the SPCA on her way in to work. But as she watched him stalk a grasshopper through the dandelions, she thought maybe she ought to take him to the vet instead.

The last thing you need is a pet, the voice of reason sounded in her head.

That was probably true, but it was nice to wake up this morning with company. Her kids were grown, and her husband had left her for someone more compliant years ago. Most of the time, she didn't mind. It was good to be alone, to have time to decompress. Real crime scenes were not like TV ones, and there were sights that could not be unseen. But while she could talk to her potted rubber tree without having to filter anything, it was also true that it never responded to her touch or made any attempt to show affection.

"There's a little knot, here between the shoulder blades. Could be from vaccinations, but I can't be sure. Why don't we give Gato a booster, just to be safe, and quarantine him for ten days? Then you take him home and keep him confined for another thirty-five days. Do not let him outside, and do not let him be around other animals. If you take him to a shelter, they will almost certainly euthanize him. They don't have the facilities for a rabies quarantine," Dr. Anderson told Quetzel, after the detective had explained that the kitten had been found at a crime scene where the suspect was infected with rabies. "If you notice any changes in behavior at all," the doctor continued, "like aggression, loss of appetite, or lethargy, bring him in immediately."

"How can you tell if a cat is being lethargic?" Cazares asked. She was only half joking.

The vet laughed. "At this age, and I would say he's three to four months old, he should be pouncing on anything that moves. When he's not napping."

Cazares was reluctant to leave the kitten, but it was only for a week and a half. "I'll see you soon," she told him. Then she left to get her own rabies vaccination.

🐈

Trunk bodies during the summer were the worst. It was not possible to get used to the sickly-sweet smell of rotting blood, or the pungent stench of decaying flesh. But Cazares had found that shallow breaths through her mouth lessened the impact.

The corpse had been ripening for at least a week in the full sun. Cazares scowled as she stepped in a puddle of vomit near the car. Several travelers had reported a foul smell coming from the sedan, which had been sitting in the Park and Ride lot at the airport for eight days, according to the gate ticket. Security had called the police, and the responding patrol officer had not responded well to the horror show in the trunk.

It was impossible to tell by looking at the putrefying body whether it had been male or female. The clothes suggested male. The corpse was too friable to search where it was, so Cazares didn't know if there was a wallet. But the papers in the glove compartment showed that the late model car had been rented to one Mateo Fuentes, and there was a ten-day-old boarding pass in the same name for a flight from Madrid, Spain to Houston.

At least one blue bottle fly had found her way into the trunk, probably attracted by the small pool of blood which had dripped out of the trunk vent and down the inside of the tire. Not only was the festering corpse alive with fat, white maggots, but brown pupa cases dotted the interior of the trunk. The forensic bug guys could get a pretty good time of death. It was not obvious whether the decedent had been dead when the trunk was locked, or shut in there and left to die. Ultimately, that would only matter to the District Attorney, when she was deciding what charges to file.

There wasn't a lot more Cazares could do at the scene, so while she was waiting for the Medical Examiner to figure who the decedent was and how he got to be a decedent, she would see what she could find out about Mateo Fuentes.

She started at the car rental agency.

When the counter agent pulled the lease records, she gave Cazares the name and contact information for the graveyard shift agent from that date. Quetzel saw no reason for delay, and she called immediately.

"Hello?" a sleepy voice rasped.

"Sorry to wake you up. Am I speaking with Harry Frampton?"

"Who wants to know?"

"Detective Cazares. I'm investigating a homicide. I need to ask you some questions about a man who leased a car last week."

"Um. Yeah. Sure. What happened?"

"Sunday morning, a week ago, someone named Mateo Fuentes rented a maroon Hyundai HB20 at 1:45 AM. Do you recall renting that car?"

Frampton barely paused. "Oh, I remember that guy. It was a really slow night - he was the only one who came in.

He had little wire-framed glasses and a huge nose. Made me think of a bird."

"Was he alone?"

"He came in to the counter alone. There was some chick waiting outside with his luggage, though."

A disheveled family came in to pick up their rental. The mother's eyes widened as she caught sight of Cazares' gun and she pulled her toddler close to her. Quetzel retreated to the far corner of the lobby.

"Can you describe her?" she asked Frampton.

"Not really. She had on a big flowered-y hat. Short shorts and a tramp stamp. She kept her back to the door, though."

"What about the tattoo? What did it look like?"

"She was too far away. I could see she had some ink, but I couldn't really tell what it was."

"Did Mr. Fuentes seem agitated, or did he say anything unusual?"

"No, I don't think so."

"Ok, Mr. Frampton, thanks for your help. I'm going to leave one of my cards here at your work. If you think of anything else, please call me."

"Sure."

As she was ending the call, the manager strode out of the back room. "Can I help you with something?" he asked.

His shoulders were pulled back, forcing his chest out, and his tone was bordering on gruff. Claiming his territory, no doubt.

Quetzel smiled and held out her hand. "I'm Detective Cazares."

The manager took her hand to shake.

"One of your rental cars was discovered at the airport with a corpse in the trunk," Cazares continued.

Color drained from his face as if someone had pulled a plug somewhere down in his belly. He quickly retracted his hand. "We run a respectable business here. Nothing like this has ever happened to us."

"Nothing like that had ever happened to your client, either."

The color returned to the manager's face. "Of course not. It's very tragic for his family. Or her?"

"The lessee was male. Not sure about the body."

The manager turned slightly green.

🐈

"*Buenas noches*!" Mateo Fuentes said to his computer monitor. He glanced up over the top of the screen. "Wait."

He put down his headset and got up. The door to his study had opened slightly. He looked into the dark hallway, and listened for a moment. It must have been a draft – his wife and children did not appear to be stirring.

"Sorry," he said, replacing the headset.

"No problem!" the young woman on the other end of the video chat gushed.

She wore a tight white tank top that left nothing to the imagination, and her hair was pulled back, clipped messily to her head. As if she'd just rolled out of bed.

"Are you ready to practice your English?" she asked, giggling.

"Yes, yes. Very much, Rhonda."

Rhonda leaned forward, clearing the view straight down the middle of her low-cut top. "I love the way you say my name. Your accent is so sexy."

Mateo laughed nervously. His eyes flickered to the closed study door. "You are the sexy one."

Rhonda batted her eyelashes and beamed. "So when are you coming to the States? I can't wait to give you a tour of Houston. You said you would visit. Maybe after that, you could give me a tour of Spain."

"I sometimes have business trips to Los Angeles. I will tell my wife that is where I am going. Two weeks from today, I will be with you."

Rhonda's mouth curled into a sympathetic smile, and she shook her head. "I don't understand what is wrong with your wife. If I had such a strong, sexy man in my bed, I'd never ignore him."

Her fingers absently fingered a gold pendant around her neck. It was a maneki-neko, a beckoning cat, that she always wore because it was supposed to bring good fortune. She'd found it on eBay and bought it for herself on her birthday years ago, she'd told Mateo.

Mateo avoided any mention of his four children, as he sat at his desk, chatting with the woman probably young enough to be his daughter. The baby wouldn't wake to be fed until around two AM, so as long as he slipped into bed with his wife by one thirty, he should be safe. It was 12:45 when Rhonda casually began to rub her left nipple through her shirt. Mateo's cock leapt to attention, and he was glad he'd already slid his pants down around his ankles. Just as he reached for the half-empty bottle of lotion near the computer, Mateo Junior began to wail from his crib.

"I call you back tomorrow," he hissed before hastily shutting down the internet browser and scrambling to pull his clothes back on.

When she was at the car rental agency, Cazares had taken photocopies of Mateo Fuentes' identification. He was a manager at a large textile company. There was a seven-hour time difference between Houston and Madrid, so the company had been closed for hours, even taking the afternoon siesta into account. Didn't matter. The police station was always open.

Quetzel's father was originally from Guatemala, and she'd grown up speaking both Spanish and English. The language would be easy. The conversation would not.

After spending twenty minutes either being transferred or sitting on hold, she finally spoke with an Inspector Allende at Police Station Luna in Madrid. Mateo Fuentes' wife had reported him missing after he'd left for a business trip to Los Angeles, California, ten days ago and seemingly dropped off the face of the Earth. She'd been unable to reach him by phone or email, and none of his business contacts had heard from him or seen him. He always took the 1:00 PM flight on Saturday afternoon when he traveled to Los Angeles. Not only had he not boarded, he didn't even have a reservation. The Inspector believed that Fuentes was playing hooky from his family, and would return soon, unaware that he'd been caught out.

Cazares hoped she had all the details right. Guatemalan Spanish was not the same as Castilian Spanish. But it was probably close enough.

"I have a John Doe in the trunk of a car rented to a Mateo Fuentes who lives on Calle de Gomez Ortega, in Madrid, Spain," Cazares told Allende in Spanish.

He *tsked*. "Can you send me his finger prints?"

"Too decomposed. I can send you X-Rays of his mouth for his dentist to look at. Otherwise, if you can obtain a sample, maybe swab one of his kids, we can run DNA."

The Inspector paused. Perhaps he was weighing the cost of expensive DNA tests against the glory, or at least good PR, of solving the case. "I can do that," he said at last.

For her part, Quetzel was relieved she didn't have to break the news to Fuentes' widow. That was the very worst part of her job.

Rhonda hadn't really needed the sign when Mateo arrived at Terminal E early Sunday morning. It had read, "Señor Caliente" on hot pink poster board that matched her barely-there pink shorts. If she hadn't been wearing the necklace with the gold, waving cat, Mateo might not have recognized her at first. She was wearing a flower print bucket hat that hid most of her face. She led him to the rental car agency shuttle. She had sat almost in his lap on the bus, but she waited outside with his luggage while he signed all the papers. As soon as his suitcase was in the back of the car, she planted a big sloppy wet kiss on his mouth. He responded eagerly.

"Not here," she said with a grin, nodding toward the rental office. "My apartment."

They made pointless small talk, and he stroked her inner thigh as she drove. It took half an hour to get to her place, and he was ready for action as soon as the door closed behind him.

What he got was action of a completely different sort. A very large man, six and a half feet, if he was an inch, stood up from the couch.

"What is this?" Mateo asked, indignant.

"This is Bear. He's my boyfriend." Rhonda replied.

"Your boyfriend? I thought..."

"Oops," she said, putting her hand to her lips in mock surprise. "He's also my business partner."

"*Puta*! You lie to me!" Mateo growled.

"I lied to you? Maybe we should call your wife and see what she thinks about that." Rhonda pulled the cellphone out of her purse.

Mateo lunged at her, snatching at the device. Bear stepped in and grabbed Mateo by the hair on the back of his head. Mateo tried to twist away from him, but Bear pulled back, hard. There was a sickening crunch as Mateo's neck snapped, and he went limp.

"Ohhhh! Really? Did you have to go and kill him? Idiot! Now we can't get his PIN numbers." Rhonda glared at Bear. "I hope you know how to clean up this mess."

Bear put on a pretend pout. "This is hardly any mess. Let me show you something really messy."

He let go of Mateo's hair, and he slumped to the floor. Bear reached out with a big paw, grabbed Rhonda around the waist, and kissed her hard. She murmured with pleasure.

Mateo lay on the floor. He couldn't speak. He could move nothing but his eyes. He closed them, and focused on trying to breathe, while the animal sounds of the writhing couple on the floor a few feet away from him drowned out the niggling voice of regret inside his head. He wondered what his wife would tell Mateo Junior about his father.

"It'll be light soon" said Bear. "We'd better get him out of here. Probably a lot of people look at apartments on Sunday."

Rhonda nodded. She sat up and pulled on her top. Her eyes fell on Mateo, and she cursed under her breath.

"Bear! He's not dead."

The big man got up and pushed Mateo's arm with his big foot, then watched the paralyzed man's eyes dart fearfully in his head. Bear shrugged.

"He will be soon."

Bear pulled on some driving gloves and picked up an old quilt from off the floor. It had a slimy spot on it from the couple's earlier romp. He hummed to himself as he fished the car keys and wallet out of Mateo's pockets, then wrapped him up in the blanket. While Bear carried Mateo down to the car and put him in the trunk, Rhonda put on kitchen gloves and made sure everything in the apartment was exactly as it was when they broke in. She knew the furnished apartment was empty, because the leasing agent had shown it to her on Friday. Rhonda just needed a place for a quick shakedown, and vacant apartments worked great for that. Mateo wasn't the first, and wouldn't be the last. But he was the first to die. Most of the time, the would-be boyfriends coughed up their cash and went slinking back to their wives. It was his own fault, she told herself. If he hadn't been talking to strangers on the internet, cheating on his wife, this would never have happened to him. She could hardly be blamed for passing up a business opportunity.

When Bear got back, Rhonda removed the baggage tag from Mateo's suitcase and went out the front door with it. Bear locked the door behind her, then crept out through the rear sliding glass door. They drove Mateo's rental car to the airport Park and Ride lot and parked it. They had to hurry. The horizon was turning grey with the approaching dawn.

Bear pulled the blanket from around Mateo. "You'll thank me for this," he said, pulling a box cutter out of his pocket. "This will be a lot quicker than being roasted alive in the heat." He pulled Mateo's head back and covered his face with the quilt. Bear reached underneath the blanket and slashed Mateo's throat. After the initial spurt of blood, Bear pulled the quilt away.

"Ow!" he complained as he bumped his head on the locking mechanism of the trunk. He put his fingers to his head. *Good. No blood.*

Rhonda leaned in. "I'm sorry. It wasn't supposed to be this way. You weren't supposed to die."

She didn't seem to notice that the clasp of her necklace had broken, and the little gold cat tumbled into the trunk. It was quickly swallowed by Mateo's pulsing blood.

Bear slammed down the trunk lid. The quilt had caught most of the blood from the attack, and the little on his hands was easily rinsed off with a bottle of water. Then they threw the quilt in the dumpster, caught the shuttle to the airport terminal, got off at the first stop, and left Mateo's suitcase on the bus.

🐈

After Detective Cazares hung up with Inspector Allende from Madrid, she looked at Mateo Fuentes' boarding pass. She would get the surveillance video from airport security and see if anyone met him in the terminal – she just needed to know the time frame. He cleared Customs at 1:03 AM. Finally, she found it. A young woman met him in the passenger pick up area. A young woman wearing a floral print bucket hat. Why does someone wear a sun hat in the middle of the night? Perhaps because they don't want to be recognized on security cameras.

Fuentes' dentist confirmed that John Doe's X-rays matched those of Mateo Fuentes. His wife had given her husband's computer to the Madrid police, and they had also obtained his phone records. There were frequent video chat calls, but the Skype account of Fuentes' friend had been recently deleted. Inspector Allende forwarded Fuentes' texts for the last thirty days to Cazares. Most of them were ordinary. Some of them were selfies of naked breasts. Since the same piece of jewelry, a gold cat with one paw raised high, appeared in each photo, the breasts likely belonged to the same person. Cazares frowned at the photos. Not because of the bare breasts, but because of the tacky little cat pendant. Her grandmother had had one just like it, and she hated those things. She also thought it was very probable that the owner of the breasts was also the owner of a floral print bucket hat and had a tattoo on her lower back.

The alarm on Cazares' phone went off. She looked at the clock. She'd better get a move on if she was going to make it by the vet clinic to pick up Gato before 5:30. She grabbed Fuentes' file and headed for the door. She had to stop and get a litter box and cat food on the way, too.

Dr. Anderson led Quetzel to one of the exam rooms. "He seems fine, just a happy little guy. He's been eating well. If anything at all seems wrong, bring him in."

"Okay."

A tech in zebra print scrubs brought Gato into the room and set him on the table.

"Mew!" the kitten said, then began purring.

Quetzel reached out to stroke him. He purred. Gato had filled out a lot in ten days - he'd gone from having sunken flanks to a rounded belly.

The tech used a large pair of bandage scissors to remove the hospital ID collar from his neck.

"Okay, that's it," said Dr. Anderson. "He'll need to come back in eight weeks for another round of shots and worming. Make sure you bring him in immediately if he starts feeling bad or acting strangely."

"Thanks, Doc," Quetzel said.

Gato complained as she stuffed him into the pet crate she'd just bought. His claws got stuck in the pad, and for a moment, Quetzel wondered if she ought to just take him home without the crate. Nonsense. She wouldn't let her kids ride in her car without seatbelts, and they were all over twenty-one. This baby, no matter how cute, did not get to make the rules.

There was a pet door in the utility room door that opened to the back yard. It was there when Quetzel bought the house. She would have replaced the door with a more secure one, but she had toyed with the idea of getting a dog for a while now. Quetzel double-checked that it was closed and locked before she let Gato out of the crate. She wondered if it would be too big a liability with a cat. She still might get a dog someday.

Gato had been fed, and Quezel would make herself a sandwich in a little bit. She sat on the couch, sifting through the crime scene photos one after another, staring at each in turn. There was something odd about the blood clots in the trunk, something wrong enough to catch her attention, but not so wrong as to be obvious. She could connect the woman with the big hat to Mateo Fuentes, but she could not connect her to the crime scene. It was possible she was not involved. The Medical Examiner's report showed that the cause of death was a blood loss from a deep laceration that transected the entire coronal plane of the laryngopharynx. Fuentes' tox screen had come back clean, and Cazares doubted that Miss HotPants could wrestle him into the trunk of his car and slash his throat, especially not with enough force to break his neck. Not without help, anyway.

"Mew."

Quetzel looked at the little black kitten. Since he'd been cleaned up at the vet's, she noticed that he had a little white spot on his chest, the size of a dime, maybe smaller.

He twisted his head to the side when she looked at him, then raised his left paw.

"What are you, a maneki-neko?"

Cazares' mother was Japanese, by way of Peru, and her grandmother Akari had a hoarder-worthy collection of ceramic maneki-neko, even a few pieces of maneki-neko jewelry. The beckoning cats were supposed to bring good fortune, but Quetzel had never noticed that they had done her grandmother any particular favors. Quetzel had been the one tasked with disposing of all of the figurines when Akari died. While it had occurred to her to toss them all in the trash, she knew that would be unforgivably disrespectful to her grandmother. So she sold them all on eBay and donated the money to Akari's favorite charity, a pet rescue. It still made her shudder every time she went into a restaurant with one of those things by the cash register.

But now she knew what was wrong with the blood in the trunk.

She looked at the clock. It was nearly 6:30. Paul, one of the forensic techs who was working on the Fuentes case, would probably still be there. She called his cell.

"This is Paul."

"Hey. Are you still at the lab?"

"Just about to leave. What can I do you for, Quetzel?"

"I was looking at these photos of the trunk in the Fuentes case. There is a big blood clot near the trunk latch with kind of a funny shape. Could you look at it and tell me if there's anything inside it."

"Inside it?"

"Yeah. Like a little bracelet charm, something like that."

"Give me a few. I'll call you back."

Twenty minutes later, Cazares' phone rang.

"How did you know?" Paul asked. "There was a little gold cat, like the ones you see at Chinese restaurants, completely encased in the clot."

"Thanks, Paul. I owe you a coffee."

Cazares hung up. The gold cat was only circumstantial evidence, it was true. But it was enough to tell her she was on the right track. Putting a name and an address to Miss HotPants was the next challenge.

Three days later, Cazares' phone rang. "Quetzel? Paul."

"What have you got for me?"

"There were three hairs caught in the locking mechanism of the trunk. Got lucky - they all had follicle tissue. Even luckier, we got a DNA hit on the tissue. Belongs to one Jeremiah Quincy Jones, a frequent recipient of the county's hospitality."

Jeremiah "Bear" Jones was not difficult to track down. He tended to hang out at a grimy pool hall near the airport, and that was the first place the warrant team looked. They didn't have to go any further. He confessed and turned on Rhonda at the first whiff of a plea deal. She, however, proved to be somewhat trickier to locate.

"What are we going to do about Miss HotPants, huh, Gato? She's not going to think twice about killing anybody now, since it seems to have worked for her this time."

The kitten purred in her lap as she stretched on the couch and studied the latest mugshot of Rhonda Catherine Clark. She'd been arrested so many times for solicitation that she was probably on a first-name basis with the staff at Mykawa jail.

"Think I've had it for the night. I'm going to brush my teeth."

Quetzel set the photo down on the coffee table, and the kitten down on the sofa. Once she had left the room, Gato made the short leap from the chair to the table. He sat on the picture of Rhonda Clark, patting her cheek with his paw. His eyes glowed green, just for a moment, and he licked his lips.

Quetzel woke with a start. She listened intently in the dark, her heart thudding against her ribs. This was the second time she'd been awoken by a noise tonight. She thought she'd heard a clank or rattle, but there had been nothing out of place. Perhaps she'd dreamed it.

There it was again.

It sounded like someone was shuffling papers somewhere in the house. Quietly, she eased open the nightstand drawer and pulled out her pistol. She crept down the hall until she reached the living room. There was no flashlight beam, no shapes moving in the dark. Curious.

She snapped on the light and looked left, then right, leading with the gun. "Who's there?"

"Mew."

Gato blinked in the sudden brightness as he emerged from the hooded litter box in the utility room. The breath Quetzel had been holding escaped with a big whoosh. As she bent to pick the kitten up, she noticed that the peg that kept the doggie door from opening was half-way out. She pushed it back in, pulling the chain that kept it attached to the door taut.

"Have you been playing with this chain, Mr. Gato? Bad kitty."

She cringed. His feet were wet, and cat litter was stuck halfway up his short legs. No telling what that liquid was. She blotted his paws with a paper towel.

Quetzel checked the rest of the house, just to be sure. But there was no one besides her and the kitten. It was only half an hour before she had to get up, and after that adrenalin jolt, she was wide awake. May as well go in a little early. On her way out to the car, her phone rang.

"Morning, Quetz," Cooper Morgenstern, from the Medical Examiner's office said.

"A DB already? I haven't even made it to the office."

"Thought you needed to see this. You know that Rhonda Clark you've been looking for? Somebody found her dead in a ditch this morning. 'Bout a mile from your house. Looks like she got mauled by a wild animal."

Mrs. Comstock's Killer Pansies

"Those pansies would eat you if they got half a chance," Mrs. Comstock said to Mia, the neighbor's preschooler.

"Mom," Rob said, hand reaching for her shoulder. He was only thirteen, but he was almost as tall as his father.

"Well, it's true. They love bloodmeal and bonemeal. That's what you have to feed them to get them looking so good."

"Okay, thanks," Mia's mom replied as she herded her child away from Mrs. Comstock and down the sidewalk. She glanced over her shoulder, once, as they hurried away.

"She did ask," Mrs. Comstock said.

"Mom, that kind of talk creeps people out. They're starting to think you're weird."

Rob went back into the house, leaving Mrs. Comstock to crumble the dirt from around the flowers and sprinkle it back into the bed.

"At least you were able to do something good with your life," she muttered.

The funeral had been eight days ago. Rob seemed to be coping with the death of his best friend, Liam. But Mrs. Comstock remembered how pale her son had looked, all dressed in his black suit. How easily it could have been him in that casket instead.

"Maybe some of the choices you made weren't entirely your fault. But Rob will be okay. Rob is safe." She sprinkled more dirt on the flowers.

After a while, Mrs. Comstock went inside and took a shower. The spicy smell of the shampoo made her feel clean, and the warm water ran over her body and down the drain, taking all of her impurities with it. Lately, she took three, sometimes four, showers a day.

When she was dried off and dressed, she went into the kitchen for something cool to drink. Rob was in the den, playing his Xbox. The second controller was sitting on the couch next to him, where Liam should be sitting.

Poor, dear Liam. He had been a good kid. He had always been on the slight side, so it didn't take long for the crystal meth to ravage his body. In two months, he was gaunt and hollow-eyed, with sores on his face and arms. He had become a completely different person, a haunted boy. Mrs. Comstock had even happened upon him sitting on the floor near her purse. When he noticed her looking at him, he licked his lips and skulked away, unable to meet her eyes.

And then he was dead. The trash collectors found him in an alley, propped against a wall next to a dumpster, a syringe in his open hand and his hazel eyes staring at the graffitied wall across from him. His fourteen-year-old heart had stopped.

Rob had taken it hard. Mrs. Comstock wondered if he knew all along how Liam's story would end. Perhaps he did, but hoped for something different. Maybe there was something she could have, should have done. But she didn't know what it was. *Rob is safe, now*, Mrs. Comstock told herself. *Rob is safe.*

Mr. Comstock made it home in time for dinner, for a change. They talked about day-to-day trivia, nothing that really mattered. When Rob had excused himself from the table, Mr. Comstock said, "Have you heard anything more about that Amber Alert?"

"You mean for the eighth grader, what was his name? Tony? No, I haven't heard anything else about him."

"Bad business, bad business. What's the world coming to, when kids just disappear off the face of the earth? I hope they find whoever took him, and they get what they deserve."

"Yes. It's a terrible shame," Mrs. Comstock replied. Her skin was itchy, dirty. Even if only she could see it.

"Are you feeling okay? You look a little pale."

"I'm fine. Just tired."

As Mrs. Comstock took another shower, she thought of the morning Liam had been found. She had picked up Rob at school just before lunch. They sat in the car and talked.

She asked him if he knew who had sold the drugs to Liam. She drove around the corner a little, so they could see the common area of McLemore Middle School, where the kids hung out at lunch time.

"That's him, in the red shorts. Think his name's Anthony, but I'm not exactly sure."

It was hardly any time at all when another boy hi-fived Anthony and then suddenly bent to tie his shoe.

"Are you sure?"

"I guess so. Everybody body calls him the Candyman. If you want something, he can hook you up," Rob said. "That's what I hear, anyway," he added quickly.

Mrs. Comstock's eyebrow raised itself ever so slightly. *How closely acquainted was Rob with this Candyman?* She swallowed hard, as the image of Liam, cold and dead in his casket, arose in her mind. She had to protect Rob, and she had an idea about how to do it.

"Rob, do you think you could invite that boy over to play your Xbox or something tomorrow?"

"I have Tae Kwon Do tomorrow," Rob frowned.

"I know you do. I just want to have a little talk with him."

"Right." He rolled his eyes. "You aren't going to do something embarrassing, are you?"

Mrs. Comstock gave him a tight-lipped smile, the kind that meant he had no choice. "I can ask," he said.

The next afternoon, a surly eighth grader sat across the kitchen table from Mrs. Comstock. "Won't you have some lemonade, dear?"

The boy slugged down half the glass and pounded it down on the table, then gave an irritated sigh as big drops of it sloshed out on his hand.

"Cookie?" Mrs. Comstock held out a plate of warm chocolate chip cookies. She smiled as she studied a jagged scar on his forehead.

Without a word, the boy snatched three of them.

Don't people teach their children manners anymore?

"Now, dear, I have been told that you are selling crystal methamphetamine to the children at McLemore Middle School. Is this true?"

"I don't know what you're talking about." Cookie crumbs fell out of his mouth and scattered on his shirt.

Mrs. Comstock's jaw clenched, but she didn't speak. She took a photograph out of the pocket of her starched white apron. "Do you know this boy?"

"Maybe. I dunno."

"I think you did know him. His name was Liam. He was a good kid. But he's dead now. You sold him the drugs that stopped his heart. You killed him."

"I ain't done nuthin'."

"I'm so sorry, dear, but selling drugs to children in this neighborhood is just unacceptable. It must be stopped."

The boy snorted as he got out of the chair. But his legs collapsed, and he sprawled on the floor.

"That'll be the lemonade. I put enough rohypnol in there to paralyze a horse. After all, I can't have you screaming and thumping around when I put you in the deep freeze. You might damage the door. Besides, what would the neighbors think about all that noise? This is a respectable neighborhood, you know."

🐾

The next morning, after Mr. Comstock had left for work and Rob had gone to school, Mrs. Comstock took off her crisp apron and put on some well-worn overalls with paint splattered on them. Then she pulled on rubber kitchen gloves and dragged the frozen boy to the backyard, where the wood chipper and several five-gallon buckets were waiting. She undressed him and put his clothes in a plastic bag. She'd dump them in one of the clothing donation drop boxes near the grocery store later.

Mrs. Comstock pushed down the remorse that stabbed at her when she looked at the boy's face. She couldn't let herself think of him as someone's child. No, this was the subhuman slimeball who killed Liam. And he could kill any one of the other kids, even Rob, if he wasn't stopped.

She turned on the terrible machine.

In the end, she had to get a hacksaw to make the pieces small enough to fit into the chipper. Even so, she still had to push and shove to get him down. With each addition, the high-pitched hum of the wood chipper turned to a low growl as it struggled momentarily with its load. She had diluted the contents of the buckets with water before she poured them onto her flowerbeds. Next, she applied a sprinkling of lime and a thick layer of manure compost to hide any gristly bits and mask the odor. She'd barely finished in time to clean herself up before Rob got home from school.

The water went cold and Mrs. Comstock turned it off and got out of the shower. Any parent would do whatever it took to save their own child, she told herself. What she did was re-purpose an oxygen thief into useful fertilizer. It was a murder, but hardly a crime.

🐈

A month later, Mrs. Comstock was out weeding her flower beds. Her sister, who lived two doors down, came running down the sidewalk, chasing a fluffy black kitten. The cat stopped to scratch in the flowerbed with the pansies.

"Quetzel! Don't let that cat poop in my flowers!" Mrs. Comstock shouted.

Detective Cazares scooped up the kitten. "Look how little he is. He can't make that much poop. Besides, it's fertilizer, right?"

Mrs. Comstock coughed. "When did you get a cat? And why?"

"I found him a couple of weeks ago." Detective Cazares eyed the short metal sign next to the pansies. "I see you got 'Yard of the Month.' Again."

A group of a half dozen or so boys walked by on the other side of the street.

Mrs. Comstock glowered at them. "Those thugs. They'll be the death of this neighborhood. Selling their drugs and strutting around with their pants hanging off their hips." She shook her head, disapproving.

"Have you seen them selling drugs?" Detective Cazares asked.

"Not specifically, but Rob's best friend died about six weeks ago from a drug overdose. He bought the drugs at school." She frowned again at the group of boys, thinking the pansies could do with another feeding. It would be too warm soon. For them *and* their special fertilizer.

Cazares nodded. "I didn't work that case, but I remember it. Turns out he actually got the drugs from his uncle. He committed suicide before we could arrest him. Sad, sad case."

Mrs. Comstock had stopped listening. She suddenly felt the need to take a shower.

Grow House

The 911 caller reported shots fired and smoke coming from a house in an upscale neighborhood. When the Houston Fire and Police Departments arrived on the scene and broke down the front door, they did not find any flames or gunmen.

What they did find was 1,163 marijuana plants.

The cheap, prepaid cell phone that had been used to make the call was at the end of the front walkway, cleaner than it would have been straight out of the box from the factory. Detective Quetzel Cazares had been called to the scene because, in addition to a state of the art indoor pot nursery, there was a body.

The young man hadn't been dead for very long. He was still warm, and rigor mortis hadn't set in yet. If not for the huge, bloodless gash across his lower rib cage, he could have been mistaken for a boy having a nap, wearing nothing but shorts on a hot day.

"We haven't found any ID," Chuck, one of the officers, said.

"Not surprising," Quetzel replied. "He's probably trafficked. Looks what, fifteen?" She shook her head as she squatted by the dead Asian boy. Her nephew, Rob, was not far off fifteen, and didn't look all that different from the victim.

She had never worked in the Narcotics Division, but she knew some of the officers. Homicide and Narcotics had a lot of mutual customers.

The house was swarming with eerily jump-suited Crime Scene Investigators, FBI, DEA and ICE officers, but the medical examiner's investigator was stuck in traffic. A young woman, wrapped in a blanket, sat bruised and crying with paramedics. She had been discovered in a closet, bound and naked.

Quetzel wanted to talk to her, see what she knew about the dead boy. But the woman didn't speak English. ICE was getting an interpreter, and they believed she was Vietnamese.

The woman, who didn't look very much older than the corpse, was delicate and very pretty, with large eyes and thick hair that was bleached from black to russet. But something was not quite right about her, Quetzel felt. Something subtle. Perhaps her features were just a little too sharp, her cheekbones a little too high. She reminded Quetzel of a painting she'd seen in a museum somewhere, or perhaps in one of Grandmother Akari's old books. On a hunch, she approached the paramedics and the young lady.

"*Kon'nichiwa*," Quetzel said. "*Onamae wa?*"

The girl stood up, the blanket falling just off her shoulders. "Oh, *kon'nichiwa. Watashi wa a* Nguyen Kit *to iimas. Anata wa nihongo ga hanasemasu ka*?"

The detective almost wished she hadn't said "good afternoon" in Japanese. Her grandmother had taught her a few words, and she'd picked up a little more while she was stationed at Kadena Air Base in Okinawa. She knew the girl said her name was "Kit Nguyen" and asked if Quetzel spoke Japanese. She spoke enough of the language to get herself in trouble, but not nearly enough to question the witness. Unless she needed to ask her for directions or inquire about the sushi menu.

Quetzel shook her head. "*Hon'no ikutsu ka no kotoba,*" she replied.

The girl pulled the blanket up over her thin shoulders and sat back down.

"She does speak Japanese," Quetzel said to the officer standing near her with a notebook. "Her name is Kit Nguyen."

At 5'4", the detective still had seven inches on the witness. But there was something spooky about her, something dangerous, and Quetzel had to force herself to walk slowly across the room, back to the corpse. She'd faced stone-cold killers before, but this felt different. The girl knew exactly what had happened to that boy, Quetzel was sure of it. Whether she had a hand in it was another matter. *Where was that interpreter?*

Cooper Morgenstern, the forensic investigator, arrived before the interpreter.

"Hey, Quetz," he said.

"Coop." Quetzel nodded.

Morgenstern didn't look old enough to have a job, much less this one. But looks could be deceiving, and Quetzel knew he was one of the sharpest investigators in the state. He gloved up, opened his toolkit, and pulled out a thermometer, which he inserted into the victim's chest. While he was waiting for the reading, he lifted one of the corpse's arms and examined the back of it. He retrieved the thermometer, and made notes on a tablet computer.

"This one's been dead about two hours, maybe less. It's pretty warm in here, but there's some lividity in the arm."

Quetzel eyed the gash. "I don't think he was killed here. That's a pretty big wound, but there's hardly any blood."

Morgenstern raised the flap of skin and peered inside, then scowled. "That's odd. Liver's missing. Huh. But if the wound was administered post mortem, there wouldn't be much blood, either."

Now it was Quetzel's turn to scowl. "Somebody killed him just to take his liver? Black market organ transplants?"

"Maybe." Morgenstern lifted the boy's eyelid. "Don't see any ligature marks, but there are some petechiae."

Quetzel leaned over to see the tell-tale pin-prick spots of blood in the whites of the eye. "He was suffocated?"

"Won't know for sure until he's on the table and the labs come back. Asphyxiation isn't the only thing that can cause it. Blood thinners, vomiting, hantavirus, childbirth – well, probably not in his case." Cooper grinned.

"You're a sick man, Coop." Qetzel tried not to smile as she shook her head.

A young woman in a business suit came in the front door and went straight for Kit Nguyen. Quetzel kept one ear tuned toward their conversation, but they were not speaking a language she understood. She supposed it was Vietnamese. While she didn't understand the words, she tried to monitor the tone and timbre of Kit's voice while also listening to Morgenstern's running commentary on the corpse.

There was some flaky material, probably a dried viscous liquid around his nose and mouth. Morgenstern also found three coarse, yellow hairs, possibly dog, on the boy's shorts. It may or may not mean anything. There were certainly no dogs at the house now.

Uniforms had already canvassed the neighborhood. It was during the day and most people were at work. The few that were at home had seen nothing. One lady reported that the house had been a foreclosure, and she just assumed someone had bought it from the bank and moved in. There had been a lot of work done to it about a month ago.

Quetzel had noticed a security camera at the exterior of the front door when she came in, so she went to find out who thought they were in charge. Who knew if FBI and DEA were going to play nice about jurisdiction? She just wanted to get what she needed before it got locked down in a territorial squabble.

She noted a clump of FBI agents. One was talking and the others were doing. She approached the one who had been doing the talking.

"Hey, have your guys found the surveillance system? There's a camera at the front door, probably the back, too. I'd like to see if anybody came in or out in the last couple of hours."

"Upstairs, back bedroom," he said before turning away to take a call on his cell.

The interpreter was still talking to Kit, and Quetzel wanted to make sure she had a chance to interview the witness while she was still on-site.

"I'm detective Cazares," she said to the woman in the business suit. "I need to ask her some questions, please."

"Of course."

"First of all, is she okay? Was she assaulted?"

"She is upset and frightened, but unhurt."

"Good. I need to know who that boy was and what happened to him."

The interpreter spoke to Kit, and she replied.

"His name was Bao Pham. She only met him two weeks ago, when the triad brought them both over to take care of their plants. He was a farm boy, but she does not know where his people are from. She was just getting out of the shower when someone grabbed her, zip-tied her wrists and threw her in the closet. She didn't see who it was, other than he had on brown shoes."

"Does she have any idea who might have done this? Robbery doesn't seem to be a motive – they left all the plants."

The interpreter spoke, and Kit shook her head.

"She knows nothing."

"Ask her," said Quetzel, pausing to find the softest words possible, "if there is any significance to stealing someone's liver."

The interpreter did a double take. "I'm sorry - did you say stealing someone's liver?"

"Yes."

Quetzel watched the girl's face when the interpreter asked her the question. Kit glanced up at the detective, and Quetzel thought there was a flicker of amusement in her face. Then she spoke earnestly to the translator.

"She says that such a thing is madness, and she doesn't know why anyone would do something like that. It's horrifying."

That little micro-expression before she started talking to the translator made Cazares more convinced than ever that Kit knew a lot more than she was telling.

"I noticed you're recording that. I'd like a transcript, if you don't mind. I may need to ask more questions later." Quetzel handed the woman a card.

"Of course. Do you want an .mp3 of the recording, or a text document?"

"Both, if I can get them."

"I'll have them to you by tomorrow noon at the latest."

"Thanks."

Quetzel went upstairs to the far bedroom. Three agents were mucking around with some computers, and another two were scouring the room, looking for anything that might even remotely be considered evidence.

She knocked on the doorframe as she entered the room. "Detective Cazares, Homicide. Have you been able to look at any of the surveillance tape?"

"Yeah. Not much to see. UPS delivery about 10:30, nothing else," replied the agent who was halfway under the desk with one end of a USB cable in his hand.

"What about the back door?"

"Not a thing."

"How far back did you go?"

"Twenty-four hours."

"What about windows? Are they wired?" It wouldn't be the first time a crook had climbed through a window.

"All the first-floor ones have eyes and alarms."

"Thanks."

Unless the alleged attackers were ninjas with invisibility powers, Kit was lying.

Quetzel would need to wait for trace evidence to come back from the crime lab before she could come up with a reasonable theory about how a 4'9" 85 lbs girl incapacitated a young man nearly a foot taller and 50 lbs heavier than her and removed his liver without spilling any blood. Did she slip him a roofie, or something worse? But what happened to the liver? No trace of it had turned up in the house. They even swabbed the garbage disposal, but it didn't appear to have been used in months. Quetzel shuddered and almost texted the Crime Scene Unit lead to ask if they'd checked the kitchen for fava beans and a nice chianti. Maybe Bao had died of natural causes and Kit indulged herself in a sick fantasy. Cannibalism wasn't technically illegal, and Abuse of a Corpse was only a misdemeanor. Well, that would be up to the DA, once the medical examiner was done.

The crime scene photographs were pinned to the fabric of Quezel's cubicle wall, and she stared at them, willing a clue to pop out at her. It was the three coarse hairs, though, that occupied the detective most. Had Bao just reached down to stroke a passing dog recently? Had they fallen off the UPS delivery? Or were they related to the killer in some way?

Quetzel sighed. She should have left an hour and a half ago. Her brain was fried, and besides, she had to stop by the store and get some kitten chow for Gato. He ate a mind-boggling amount of food, for such a tiny thing. Immigration was holding Ms. Nguyen, and she wasn't going anywhere anytime soon.

Cazares decided to pay her another visit on her way home. Not exactly on her way. The airport was nowhere near where she lived. She called and arranged for an interpreter to meet her at the Immigration Detention Facility. At least traffic would likely be light – it was already 8:30 PM.

"Hello, Kit." Cazares smiled as she addressed the young woman.

The on-site interpreter was an older man who made no attempt to disguise his lack of enthusiasm for this interview.

Kit nodded.

"I'm going to record our conversation, okay?"

The interpreter mumbled, his chin resting on his left hand while the fingers of his right drummed the table.

Again, Kit nodded.

"How are you doing?" Cazares asked. "Are they treating you well?"

"Yes, I am fine. But you did not come here to ask about my accommodations," she replied through the interpreter.

"That's true." Cazares smiled, an artificial, warmth-free smile. "What I really want to know is, how did you kill that boy?"

The interpreter's ears pricked up at that question, and he was suddenly interested.

Kit snorted, and her lips curled into the merest hint of a smile. "What evidence do you have that I killed poor Bao?"

Her voice seemed pleasant enough, although the interpreter's translation sounded much rougher.

Cazares knew that she was on the right track. Kit hadn't even bothered denying that she killed Bao. And, based on her reactions, Quetzel had a sneaking suspicion that Kit was only pretending she didn't understand English.

"All of the doors and windows had cameras. No one came in or out of the house that day. Unless there's a secret passage you care to tell me about, the only one in the house with Bao when he died was you."

Kit's eyes narrowed for a split second. She paused, considering her options. Finally, she said, "I was embarrassed to tell anyone, especially the men." She glanced demurely at the interpreter, then crossed her arms and looked down at the table. "There was little to do at the house, once all of the plants were tended in the morning. Bao and I, we had sex. But he suddenly collapsed. I did not know what to do. I was afraid that the triad would blame me, and I would be punished. So I tried to make it look like we had been attacked. They could not hold me accountable for that." She looked up at Cazares through her lashes as the interpreter spoke.

It was certainly a plausible explanation, whether or not it was true. Kit admitted to having sex with Bao – that could explain the dried mucous around his nose and mouth. Did she suffocate him on purpose, or was it an accident? Still, there was one little detail she left out.

"Well, that does make sense," Quetzel said, keeping her eyes on Kit. "But could you tell me what happened to his liver?"

Even before the interpreter translated, Kit did not blink. She looked so intensely into Cazares' eyes that the detective involuntarily leaned back a little. Then she looked down, hiding her face from Quetzel.

"I told you. I tried to make it look like we'd been attacked. I cut out his liver and buried it in the back yard."

Kit put her face in both hands and sobbed. Cazares would have found it more convincing if she hadn't caught a glimpse of Kit's eye, looking at her from the gaps between her fingers.

"I'll arrange to have you brought out to the crime scene tomorrow, so you can show us where you buried it. Of course, if it's not there, well, that's the kind of thing that looks pretty bad at deportation hearings." Quetzel knew full well that, according to the surveillance camera on the back door, no one had gone through it in the past 24 hours.

Cazares' tiny rescue kitten, Gato, purred as he snuggled against Quetzel's arm, his belly distended from his recent supper. Quetzel had fallen asleep in the recliner, watching Comedy Central. She'd had about eight hours' sleep over a three-night span, and she had crashed hard, once she got still. A half-eaten sandwich from the grocery's deli lay on the TV table, attesting to that.

A movement outside the window caught the cat's attention. He hissed, standing up and pinning his ears flat to his head. His fur stood on end, nearly doubling his size. All three pounds of him.

Something with glowing yellow eyes and a snout studded with sharp teeth peered back at Gato through the bay window.

In the dark, a girl giggled.

The glowing eyes disappeared from the window, and moments later, there was a scrabbling at the doggie door in the utility room. Gato tumbled out of the chair and onto the carpet. He re-fluffed his fur, especially his tail, and marched towards the noise.

Human fingers poked out from underneath the locked security plate as it bulged inward from the force being applied to it.

Gato hissed again.

The fingers stopped pushing for a moment, then started up even more urgently than before. Quetzel snored softly in the living room, unaware of the intruder.

The small hands worked their way under the plate and found the lock. Agile fingers pulled the pin and the plate slid up easily. The hands disappeared.

Within seconds, a lustrous fox stepped daintily in through the pet door. Instead of orange, her fur was golden. The kitten was so amazed that he stopped hissing for a moment. The fox sat down, and in a moment, Kit Nguyen materialized in her place.

She laughed as she stepped over Gato on her way to the kitchen. Kit searched the drawers until she located a chef's knife. She smiled at the as she made her way around the breakfast bar to the living room, and Quetzel's recliner.

"Another liver dinner. Perhaps, since I have time, I'll take her heart as well," the girl taunted the kitten. "She should not have questioned my story. I found that very upsetting. But worst of all, she had me shut up in a concrete box. That is unforgivable, and she must pay for that, little neko. No, your Detective Cazares will not be locking anyone else away."

Gato growled, long and low, the pitch decreasing as the note was drawn out. Kit turned. There was no ridiculous kitten with bottle-brushed tail sitting behind her.

Instead, there was a black cat with a small white splotch on his chest. And it was the size of an ox. Green eyes glittered with rage.

It seemed to grin as it hissed at her again. A swat from the huge paw sent the chef's knife skittering across the wood floor. Before Kit could cry out, the monster pounced on her, blade-like fangs penetrating the back of her neck and severing her spinal cord. The beast dragged her lifeless body back to the pet door where she had entered.

Quetzel gasped as she stumbled over the corpse of a fox on her utility room floor.

"How did that get in here?" She squatted and examined the bloody wound on the scruff of its neck. "Poor thing. It must have gotten attacked by something and scrambled in here to die. Although," she reached over and tested the locking panel of the doggie door, "I was sure I locked this, huh, Gato?"

The tiny kitten purred and rubbed against her ankles.

The detective put on gloves and placed the stiff body of the fox into a plastic garbage bag. "I hope it didn't have anything contagious. You just got a round of shots, so hopefully, you're okay."

Quetzel closed the door to the utility room behind her. She added the dead fox to the trash on the curb, then bleached the utility room floor and doggie door. She had just finished that when her cell rang.

"Cazares."

"This is Lieutenant Franks. Wanted to let you know there's a BOLO for your witness from the grow house yesterday."

"What? Doesn't ICE have her?"

"She escaped. She was in her cell at lights out, and was gone this morning."

"Great. I'm on my way in. Thanks for the heads up."

Cazares hung up.

"Just what I needed, Gato. The witness, whom I think is the killer, escaped last night. Everyone's supposed to be on the look-out for her, but that'll be tough. At least you're nice and safe here in the house. I won't let any bad guys get you, don't you worry."

Gato licked his paw and purred.

Monster-O-Pedia

Cat Sidhe

It is popularly believed that Roman Legionaries brought cats with them to Celtic Britain, but there is some evidence that there were already native cats, particularly in Scotland, when the Romans arrived. Cat Sidhe (Ireland), or Cat Sith (Scotland) were legendary fairy cats, which, like most fae, were arbitrarily good or evil. They were shapeshifters who typically appeared as black cats with a small white spot on their chests, but could be cow-sized, or even manifest as fireballs. Many Celtic funerary customs were designed around preventing the cat sidhe from stealing the soul of the deceased before it could be taken away by the gods. Irusan of Knowth, and Cath Palug were two infamous examples of fairy cats. Irusan, King of the Cats, was the size of a bull and lived in a cave at Knowth in fabulous style. The poet Senchan poked fun at Irusan, and vanished without a trace. The Welsh version of Palug has him terrorizing the Isle of Anglesey, where he killed and ate almost 200 warriors. The French version puts him at Mont du Chat in France, where he defeated King Arthur in a swamp battle. Modern day sightings of large, black "phantom cat" cryptids in Britain may or may not be related to cat sidhe.

Killer Strippers

In February of 2012, a stripper who went by the stage name of "Pocahontas" was arrested on capital murder charges in Houston, Texas. She and her boyfriend had a racket where she would befriend lonely men and invite them back to her apartment. Her boyfriend would be waiting there to rob the would-be lovers. One of the targets refused to cooperate and was fatally shot. For the KHOU.com news article, go here.

Kitsune

Fox spirits are commonly associated with Japan, but legends of their exploits span Asia. In China, they're called *huli jing*, in Vietnam, they are *ho ly tinh*, and in Korea, *kumiho*. They frequently take the form of beautiful young women, but it is believed that they can impersonate any human. Trickster foxes have been known to shift into a duplicate of a particular person to wreak havoc. *Zenko* are the benevolent kitsune which are associated with the god Inari. The *yako* are the naughty foxes, who range from morally ambiguous to purely evil in character. Kitsune can live for more than a thousand years, and may have up to nine tails. In some traditions, it is the consumption of human hearts and livers that give the kitsune power and longevity. The fox's most prized possession is the *hoshi no tama*, or star ball, which is thought to be a reservoir for its magic, or even contain its soul. Stealing the *hoshi no tama* from a kitsune might result in the thief having temporary power over the fox, but if the kitsune ever gets the star ball back, retribution will be swift and brutal. Likewise, kitsune will not tolerate being tethered or confined, and anyone who attempts to do this should expect a visit from a vengeful fox.

Reptilians

Reptilians (reptoids, lizardmen, draconians, sauroids) are bipedal humanoids with scaly skin and snake-like facial features. While the earliest documented modern sighting was in 1934 in Los Angeles, California, ancient Sumerian and Greek texts describe beings which have similar characteristics to reptilians. Ancient Chinese created myths of dragon kings, and the Egyptians invoked the crocodile-headed god Sobek. There is even some speculation that the "serpent" in the biblical Garden of Eden story was a reptilian. However, while no conclusive evidence of their existence has been found, theories about their origins and agendas abound. Some believe that they are space travelers from a mysterious tenth planet in our solar system, or from the Alpha Draconi star system and/or the constellation of Orion. Others hold that they evolved from dinosaurs on a separate, but roughly parallel, evolutionary timeline as humans. Still others speculate that they are just inter-dimensional fauna, native to our universe. Whatever they are, and whatever they want, reports of reptilian creatures abound in abduction phenomena recollections.

If you enjoyed this book, please consider leaving a review at the site where you purchased it. Your reviews help others find good books!

Other Titles from Black Mare Books

**Artemis Greenleaf
For Younger Readers**
Brain's Vacation
Carl the Vegetarian
Vampire
Team Smash
El Equipo Smash
Kara's Christmas Wish

**Artemis Greenleaf
For Teens and
Tweens**
Earthbound
Cheval Bayard
Confessions of a Troll
Exit Point

**Artemis Greenleaf
For Adults**
The Hanged Man's Wife
The Magician's Children
The Devil's Advocate

The Marti Keller
Mysteries Omnibus #1
Color Me Blackthorne
The Thirteenth
Summer

Coda Sterling
Dragon by Knight
Dragon Killer

Holly Dey
Puss in Space Boots

A.B. Richards
Rescue
Icebox

Anthologies
Space City 6
First Last Forever